This 2009 edition licensed for publication by Barnes & Noble Publishing, Inc.,
by arrangement with HarperCollins Publishers.

Barnes & Noble Publishing, Inc.
122 Fifth Avenue
New York, NY 10011

ISBN 978-1-4351-1359-6
Manufactured in China.
09 MCH 10 9 8 7 6 5 4 3 2 1

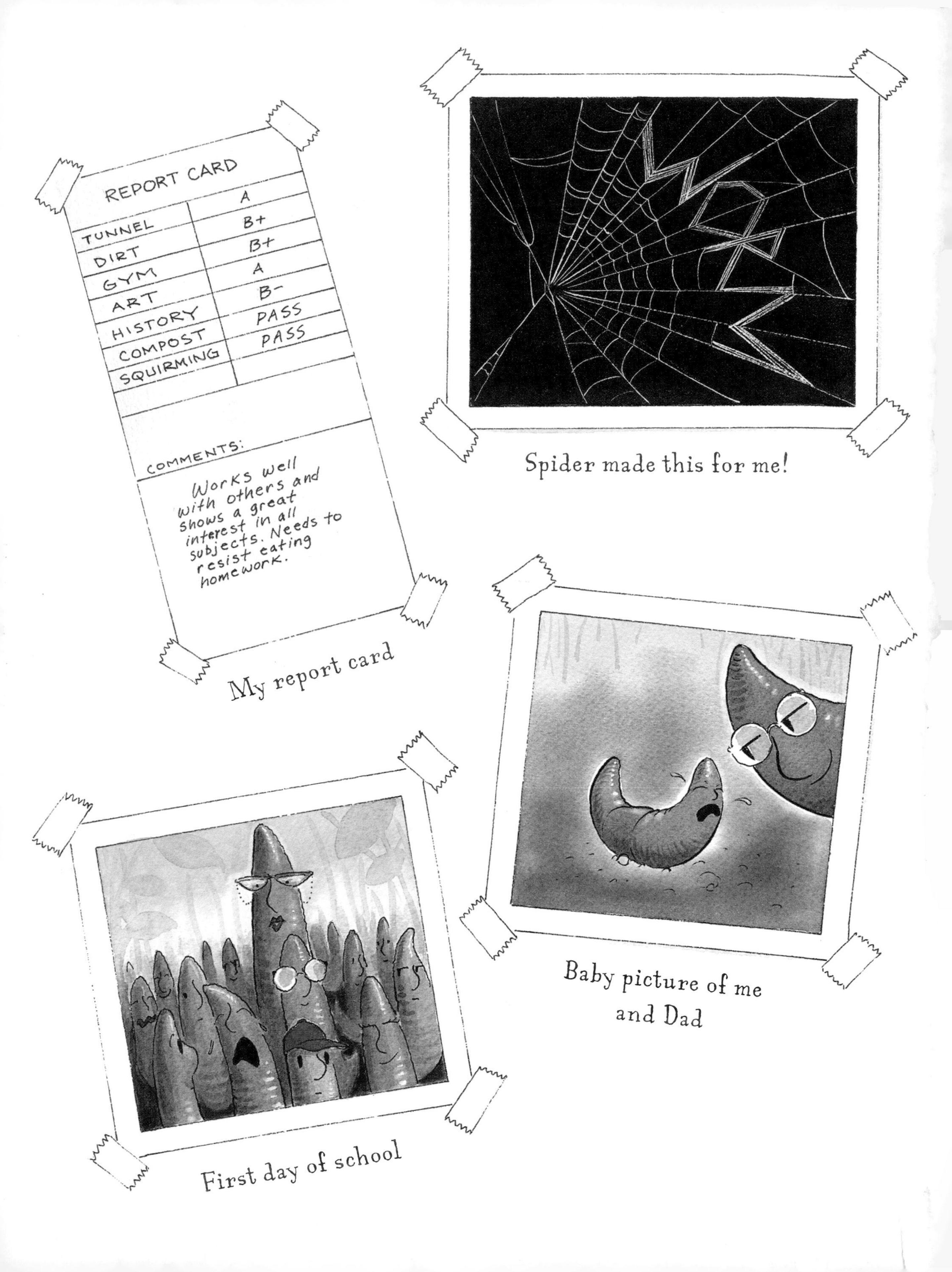

REPORT CARD

TUNNEL	A
DIRT	B+
GYM	B+
ART	A
HISTORY	B-
COMPOST	PASS
SQUIRMING	PASS

COMMENTS:

Works well with others and shows a great interest in all subjects. Needs to resist eating homework.

My report card

Spider made this for me!

Baby picture of me and Dad

First day of school

My first tunnel!
Me and Spider
The family vacation–
on Compost Island

For "the boys"–
Ken, Sean, Ryan, Patrick and Timothy
–D.C.

For Rozzie and Cheetah
–H.B.

DIARY OF A WORM

By Doreen Cronin

Pictures by Harry Bliss

JOANNA COTLER BOOKS

An Imprint of HarperCollins*Publishers*

MARCH 20

Mom says there are three things I should always remember:

1. The earth gives us everything we need.

2. When we dig tunnels, we help take care of the earth.

3. Never bother Daddy when he's eating the newspaper.

MARCH 29

Today I tried to teach
Spider how to dig.

First all of his legs got stuck.

Then he swallowed a bunch of dirt.

Tomorrow he's going to teach me how to walk upside down.

MARCH 30

Worms cannot walk upside down.

APRIL 4

Fishing season started today.
We all dug deeper.

APRIL 10

It rained all night and the ground was soaked. We spent the entire day on the sidewalk.

Hopscotch is a very dangerous game.

APRIL 15

I forgot my lunch today. I got so hungry that I ate my homework.

My teacher made me write "I will not eat my homework" ten times.
When I was finished, I ate that, too.
I will not eat
my homework. I
will not eat my
homework. I will
not eat
work. I w
my

APRIL 20

I snuck up on some kids in the park today. They didn't hear me coming.

I wiggled up right between them and they SCREAMED.

I love when they do that.

MAY 1

Grandpa taught us that good manners are very important.

So today I said "good morning" to the first ant I saw.

There were 600
more of them in line.
Good morning. Good morning. Good morning. How ya doin'? Good morning. Nice to see you. Howdy. Good morning . . .
I stood there all day.

MAY 8

Had the worst nightmare last night—

giant birds playing hopscotch.

Mom says I have to stop eating so much garbage right before I go to bed.

MAY 15

I got into a fight with Spider today.
He told me you need legs to be cool.
Then he ran. I couldn't keep up.
Maybe he's right.

MAY 16

I made Spider laugh so hard,
he fell out of his tree.
Who needs legs?

MAY 28

Last night I went to the school dance.

You put your head in.

You put your head out.

You do the hokey pokey and
you turn yourself about.

That's all we could do.

JUNE 5

Today we made macaroni necklaces in art class.

I brought mine home and
we ate it for dinner.

JUNE 15

My older sister thinks she's so pretty. I told her that no matter how much time she spends looking in the mirror, her face will always look just like her rear end.

Spider thought that was really funny.

Mom did not.

JULY 4

When I grow up, I want to be a Secret Service agent. Spider says I will have to be very careful because the president might step on me by mistake.

"It's a dangerous job,"
I told him. "But someone's
got to do it."

JULY 28

Three things I don't like about being a worm:

1. I can't chew gum.

2. I can't have a dog.

3. All that homework.

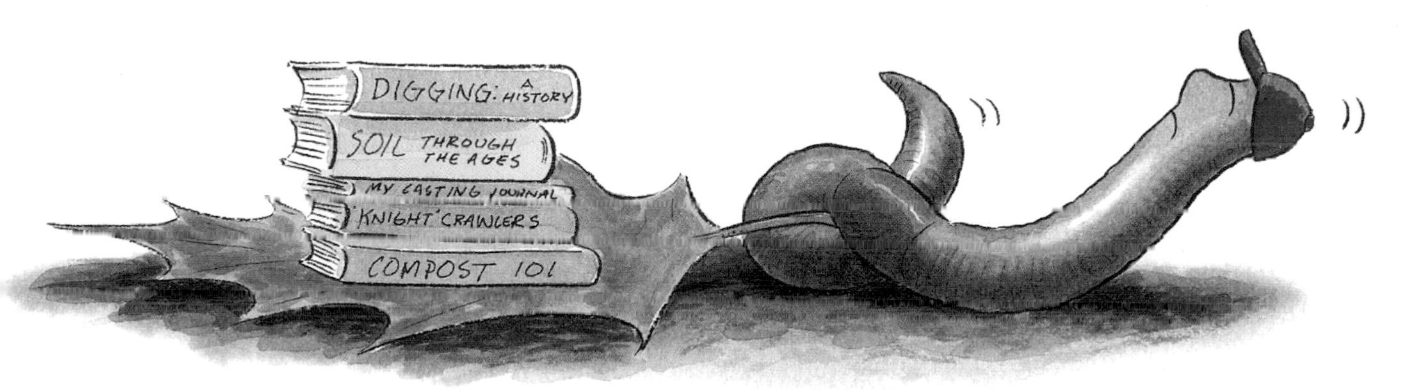

JULY 29

Three good things about being a worm:

1. I never have to go to the dentist.

2. I never get in trouble for tracking mud through the house.

3. I never have to take a bath.

AUGUST 1

It's not always easy being a worm. We're very small, and sometimes people forget that we're even here.

But, like Mom always says, the earth never forgets we're here.

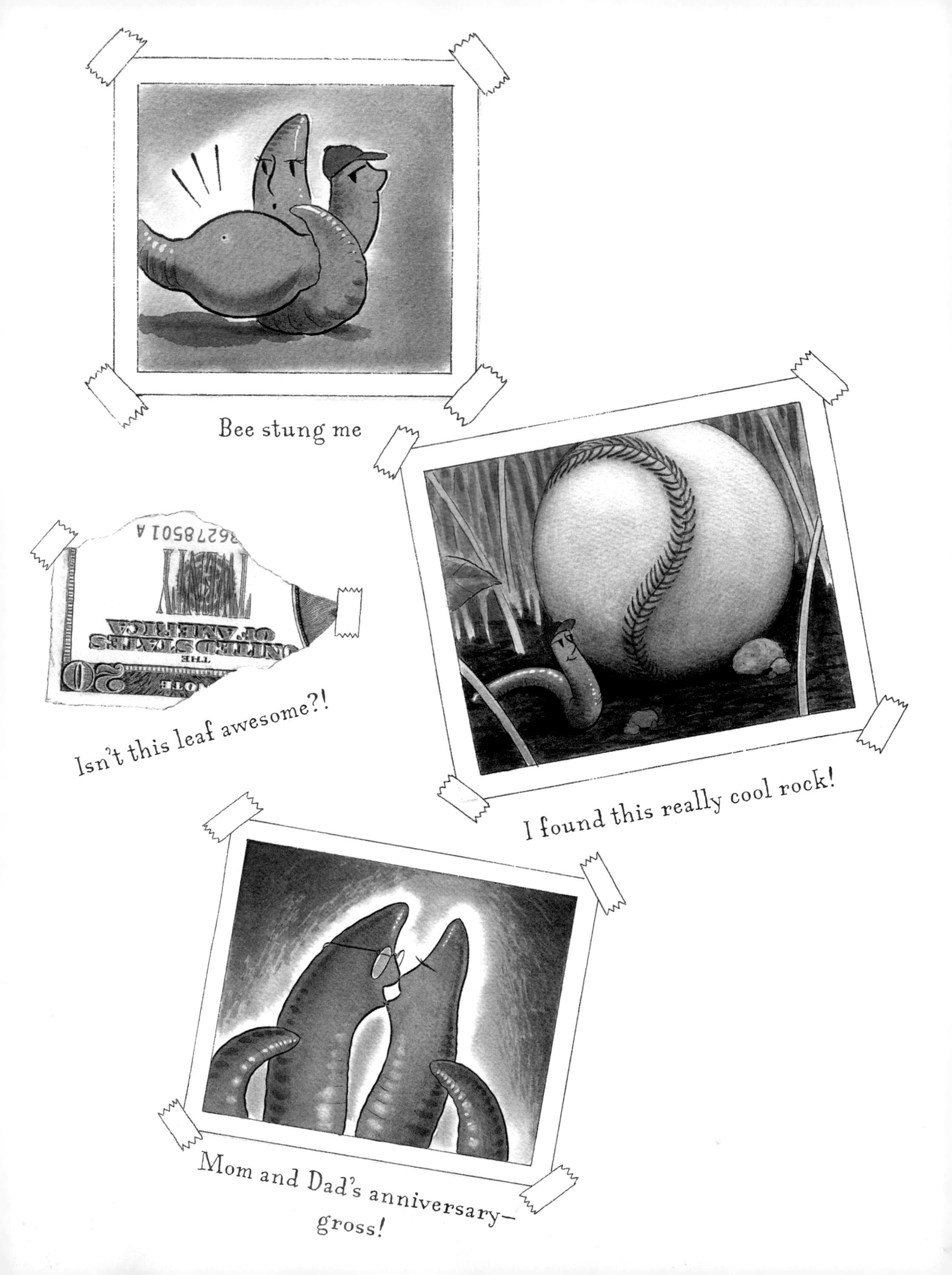
Bee stung me
Isn't this leaf awesome?!
I found this really cool rock!
Mom and Dad's anniversary—
gross!

My own comic!

My sister's slumber party (hee, hee)

My favorite pile of dirt

Cool, huh?

Family portrait

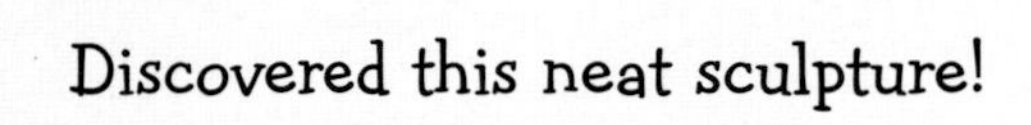

Discovered this neat sculpture!

Fly's little sister, Maggot

My first web

My favorite book, *Charlotte's Web*

Baby picture of me and Grampa

For the girls—
Meghan, Jacqueline, Theresa,
Kerry, and Amanda
—D.C.

For Valerie
—H.B.

By Doreen Cronin • Pictures by Harry Bliss

DIARY OF A SPIDER

JOANNA COTLER BOOKS
An Imprint of HarperCollinsPublishers

MARCH 1

Today was Grandparents Day at school, so I brought Grampa with me.

He taught us three things:

1. Spiders are not insects—insects have six legs.

2. Without spiders, insects could take over the world.

3. Butterflies taste better with a little barbecue sauce.

MARCH 16

Grampa says that in his day, flies and spiders did not get along.

The Compost Tim

THURSDAY APRIL 16 1971

Spiders and Flies Rumble in the City

By THE ASSOCIATED WEB

An ordinary Friday night in town turned ugly when Spiders and Flies squared off against each other in a fierce battle. Web-slinging insults of the most gruesome sort were reported from all over the metropolitan

"I've never heard such horrible name-calling in all my life," said

"I nearly broke a wing trying to fly outta there—it was

issioner Ed Grasshopper has closed Rubbish

"It's troubling for the future of

Things are different now.

MARCH 29

Today in gym class we learned how to catch the wind so we could travel to faraway places.

When I got home, I made up flash cards so I could practice:

Fly made up her own flash card:

I'm starting to see why Grampa doesn't like her.

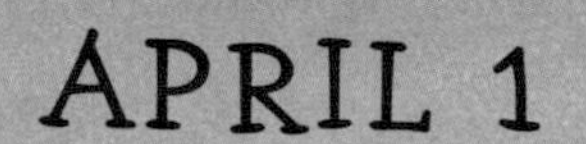

APRIL 1

Went to the park with my sister today.
We tried the seesaw.

It didn't work.

We tried the tire swing.

It didn't work.

We spun a huge sticky web on the water fountain.

That worked.

APRIL 12

Today was Safety Day at school. We learned that vacuums eat spiderwebs and are very, very dangerous.
If we hear a vacuum,
we should Stop,
Drop, and Run.

APRIL 13

We had a vacuum drill today.
I stopped what I was doing.

Forgot where I was going.

And ran screaming from the room.

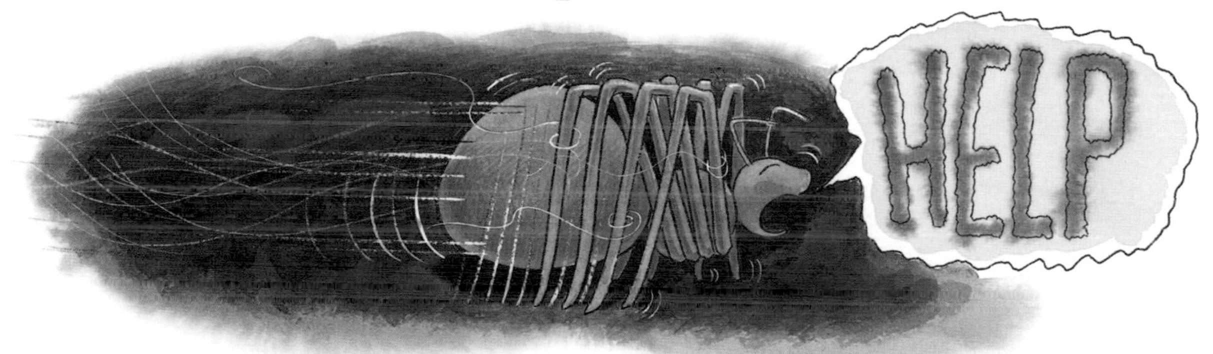

We're having another drill tomorrow.

APRIL 17

I'm sleeping over at Worm's house tonight.

I hope they don't have leaves and rotten tomatoes for dinner again.

MAY 7

Mom said I was getting too big for my own skin.

So I molted.

MAY 8

Today was show-and-tell.
So I brought in my old skin.

My teacher called on it to
lead the Pledge of Allegiance.

You there, why don't you get us started.
LOOK! U IN THE SKY. IT'S...
APTAIN UNITED!
WE'RE SAVED
??

JUNE 5

Daddy Longlegs made fun of Fly because she eats with her feet. Now she won't come out of her tree house.

I'm going to find him
and give him a piece
of my mind!

JUNE 6

I found Daddy Longlegs.

He's a lot bigger than I thought he was.

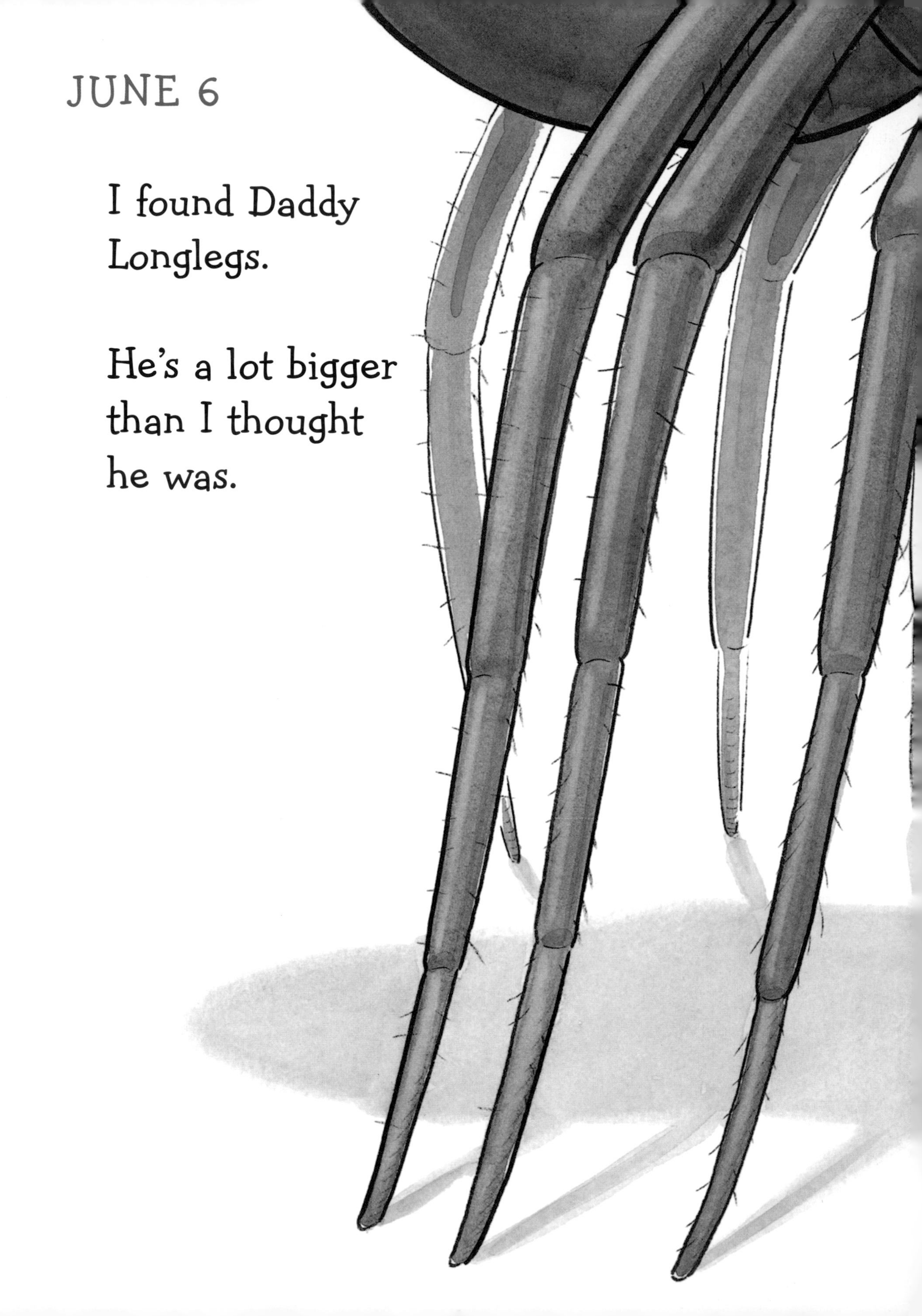

I gave him a piece
of my lunch
instead.

JUNE 7

Fly's tree house blew away in the wind today.

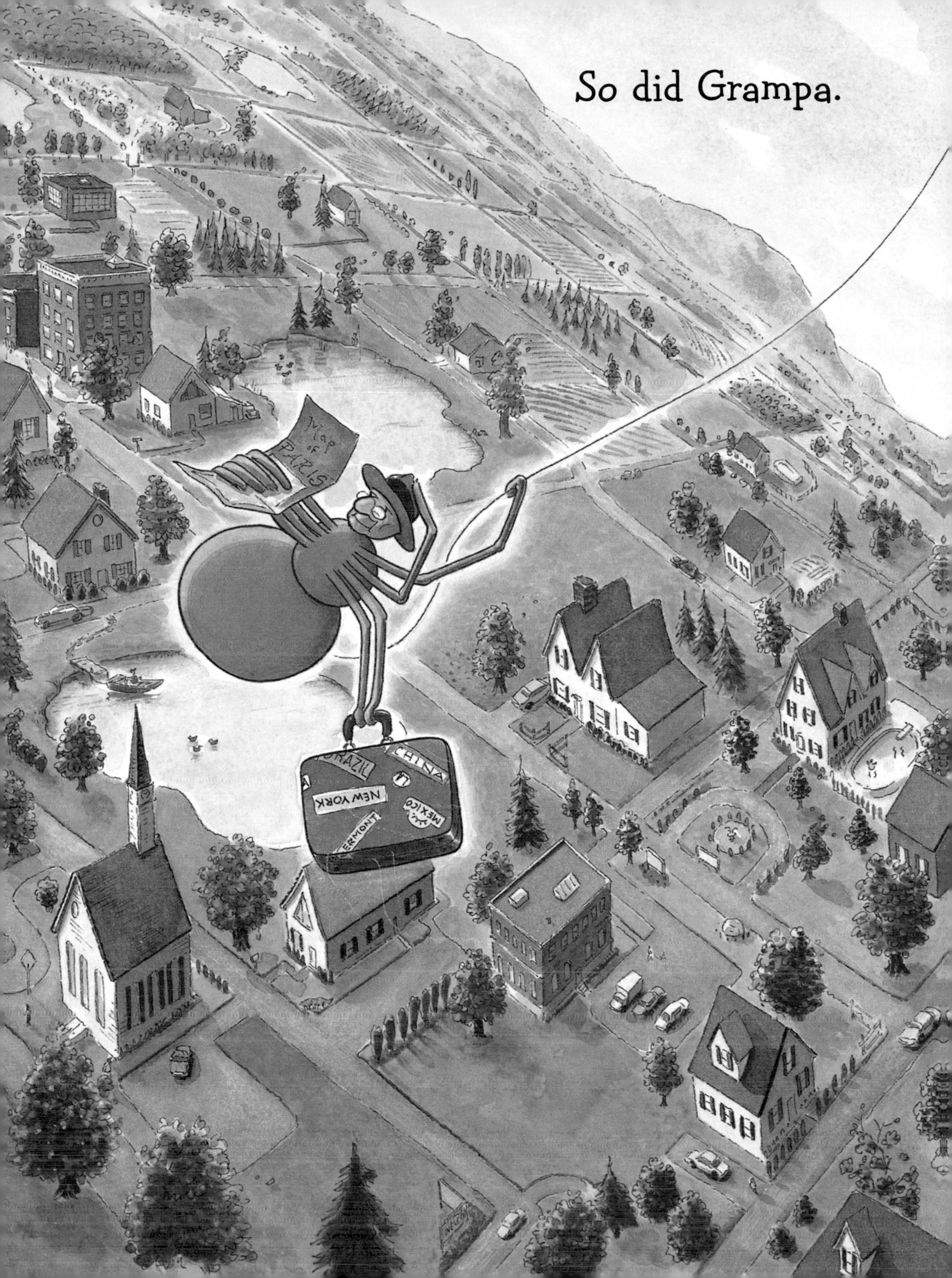

So did Grampa.

JUNE 18

I got a postcard from Grampa today:

PARIS – FRANCE

Dear Spider,
Ooh-la-la!
I landed in Paris!
French bugs are
delicious!
Au revoir,
Grampa

leg of French gnat... → give it a try!

Spider
5 Web Ave.
Arachnidville
05400
USA

Tomet co.

JUNE 30

Grampa came home today.

I couldn't wait to hear about
how he rode the winds
all the way over the ocean!

Turns out, he caught a breeze to the
airport and napped in first class.

JULY 2

Fly came over to play today. She got stuck in our web, and her mom had to come get her.

Grampa laughed a little too hard.
HAHAHAHAH
FLY
From now on,
we have to play
at Fly's house.

JULY 9

Today was my birthday.
Grampa decided I was
old enough to
know the secret
to a long, happy life:

Never fall asleep in a shoe.

JULY 16

Things I scare:

1. Fly's mom

2. Tiny bugs

3. People using water fountains at the park

JULY 17

Things that scare me:

1. Daddy Longlegs

2. Vacuums

3. People with big feet

AUGUST 1

I wish that people wouldn't judge all spiders based on the few spiders that bite.

I know if we took the time to get to know each other, we would get along just fine.

Just like me and Fly.

Dad made me this!

Worm found this!

My best friends

My first molted skin

Extended family reunion

I made this slingshot!